Jan 2005

Dear Emma,

The next time you come visit us, we can go to some of the fun places you'll learn about from this book.

Happy Birthday!

Love,
your favorite New Yorkers!
Ella, Aunt Yappy & Uncle Dieter

Libby Patala

MADISON in NEW YORK

Written by
Libby Pataki and Wilson Kimball
Illustrated by Betsy Day

Other books from VSP Books:

Woodrow, the White House Mouse, about the presidency and the nation's most famous mansion.

House Mouse, Senate Mouse, about Congress and the legislative process.

Marshall, the Courthouse Mouse, about the Supreme Court and the judicial process.

A "Mice" Way to Learn About Government, a teacher's curriculum guide for the three books above.

Woodrow for President, about how Woodrow got to the White House.

A "Mice" Way to Learn About Voting, Campaigns and Elections, a teacher's curriculum guide for *Woodrow for President.*

President Adams' Alligator and Other White House Pets, which teaches children about the presidents through their pets.

Alexander, the Old Town Mouse, about historic Old Town, Alexandria, Va., across the Potomac River from Washington, D.C.

Nat, Nat, the Nantucket Cat (with Susan Arciero), about beautiful Nantucket Island, Mass.

Nat, Nat, the Nantucket Cat Goes to the Beach (with Susan Arciero), about a trip to the beach on Nat's favorite island.

Martha's Vineyard (with Susan Arciero), about wonderful Martha's Vineyard, Mass.

Cornelius Vandermouse, the Pride of Newport (with Susan Arciero), about historic Newport, R.I., home to America's most magnificent mansion houses.

Order these books through your local bookstore by title,
or order **autographed copies** of the Barnes's books by calling **1-800-441-1949** or from our website at **www.VSPBooks.com.**

For a brochure and ordering information, write to:

VSP Books
P.O. Box 17011
Alexandria, VA 22302

To get on the mailing list, send your name and address to the address above.

ISBN 1-893622-15-0

Library of Congress Catalog Card Number: 2004108371

10 9 8 7 6 5 4 3 2 1

Printed in the United States of America

Dedication

To Emily, Teddy, Allison and Owen — L. P.

To Bradford, Justin & Lindsay — W. K.

*To Brien, Cheryl, Carrie, Eric and most of all Sergio,
my family of cheerleaders. — B. D.*

Acknowledgments

*We would like to thank Linda Langton, our agent, for her
support and dedication. We would also like to thank Cheryl and
Peter Barnes who are good friends and great editors. Lastly, we
want to thank Kimberly Cullen for entertaining us with so many
stories about her niece Madison that we couldn't name this
sweet child anything else. — L. P. and W. K.*

Literary Agency: Langtons International Agency, New York

*I want to thank Ruth Danon, who always reminds me to
trust myself and the process. — B. D.*

My name is Madison. I live in New York City in a brownstone with a garden in the back. I was in the garden blowing bubbles when my parents brought home a puppy for me on my eighth birthday. He's a Yorkshire terrier, so I named him New Yorkey.

The first thing I did when I got New Yorkey was brush out his fur, put a blue ribbon in his hair and put a blue collar around his neck. The collar has sparkly stars on it. Ever since that first day, we have been best friends. We go on long walks together all over New York.

The first place we ever walked to was the Empire State Building. It was a bright sunny day, so I bought a pair of blue star-shaped sunglasses for New Yorkey that matched my pink ones. I firmly believe you can't be too sparkly.

When we arrived at the Empire State Building, we ran into mommy and daddy's friend, Professor O'Shea. "Top of the morning to you, Madison," Professor O'Shea said. New Yorkey barked a greeting to him, "Arf, arf, arf," (which means "And the rest of the day to you"). Then New Yorkey and I went all the way to the tipity top. On a clear day, you can see all five boroughs of New York City: Bronx, Brooklyn, Queens, Staten Island and, of course, Manhattan.

Next we walked to Madison Square Garden to watch a basketball game. At the game New Yorkey learned how to do "the wave." Every time our team scored, he and I stood up and sat down with the other fans, so that it looked like we were a giant wave. Of course, no one else in the wave barked or had to stand on his hind paws.

Another time, New Yorkey and I went to see the Statue of Liberty because it's a very important landmark. I put a Statue of Liberty foam crown on New Yorkey's head. He looked just like Lady Liberty, except a lot smaller. Of course we only wear faux (which is French for fake) fur. I think faux fur is a million billion times better than real fur!

Then we took a ride on the Staten Island Ferry where we ran into my pediatrician. "Hola, Doctor Ramon, como estas?" (which means "Hello Doctor Ramon, how are you?"), we asked. Doctor Ramon replied, "Muy bien, Madison. Y tu?" (which means "Very good, Madison. And you?"). New Yorkey barked, "Woof, woof" (which means "Muy bien") and then he wagged his tail for good measure.

One day we went for a long walk through Central Park. We stopped at the Alice in Wonderland statue. I put New Yorkey on the giant bronze mushroom and looked at him through my looking glass. His eye looked very big! Then we went to the Central Park Zoo. I wanted to see the sea lions and New Yorkey wanted to see the tree frogs. Tree frog eyes are very small!

Next we went to the Museum of Natural History to see the Butterfly Conservatory. "Bonjour, Monique" (which means "Hello, Monique"), I said to the woman who always takes our tickets. "Bonjour, ma chérie" (which means "Hello, my darling"), Monique responded with a smile. As soon as we walked into the Conservatory, a Monarch butterfly landed on New Yorkey's head. When it opened its wings, it looked like New Yorkey was wearing a brown and orange barrette, which made me giggle and smile. New Yorkey was so happy that he kissed my face all over, which made me feel good all day.

After the museum, we went to Lincoln Center. There is so much to do at Lincoln Center that you could go there every night. My mother prefers opera. My father would rather watch plays. I like ballet. Before the ballet starts, I like to sit by the fountain with New Yorkey. Sometimes, like today, if we are really excited, we do a million billion somersaults all around the fountain until both of our tongues hang out.

It was nearly Christmas and *The Nutcracker* ballet was playing. I dropped New Yorkey off backstage with Mrs. Gold, the costume director. Mrs. Gold put a little blue tutu on New Yorkey and a new blue ribbon in his hair. When it was time for New Yorkey to go on stage, he danced right across the stage on his hind legs! When he got to the other side, Mrs. Gold gave him a piece of chocolate babka. He was very happy, and so was I because she kept a piece for me, too. Yum!

During the holidays, we went skating at Rockefeller Center. After he crawled into my backpack, I put New Yorkey's new blue earmuffs on his ears. While I did figure eights on the ice, he hung out of my backpack watching the world spin past him.

In the spring, I took New Yorkey to The Museum of Modern Art. He is a fan of painter Bark Roofko. Every time he sees Roofko's work, he sits in front of it until his tongue hangs out of his mouth. That night when we went home, I laid out color paint and a white canvas. New Yorkey walked through all the paint and then walked all over the canvas. Now he has his own show in a Soho gallery on Prince Street. It's called Paw Prince by New Yorkey.

New Yorkers call The Metropolitan Museum of Art the "MET" because it's short for "Metropolitan." I didn't know that when I was little. I thought it was called that because people met there to look at art. My parents met there at an event that was held in the Temple of Dendur. Now every time we go, I want to visit the Temple and have them tell me the story of how they met at The MET.

Even though New Yorkers like to walk, they take the subway sometimes.

New Yorkey and I took the
shuttle train to Times Square, a mass
of bright lights and people rushing to Broadway shows.
New Yorkey has an audition for a show called *Doggity*.

The casting director,
Mr. Mumbai, wants to see
New Yorkey roll over, balance on a
ball and play dead. After the audition, Mr.
Mumbai called my mother and said, "They
don't have dogs like this in Bollywood." I
don't know where Bollywood is but I'm sure
we will like it because we love to travel.

One warm day, we walked to Chinatown. "Ni-hao?" (which means "How are you?"), I said to Mr. Chu, who owns a store that sells fish and frogs. I wanted a frog to live in my tub and take baths with me. Yorkey doesn't like to take baths. I reached into the barrel of frogs but I couldn't catch one. Mr. Chu reached in and pulled one out. He poked its belly. The frog said, "Gribbitt, gribbitt, gribbitt" (which means "My name is Fred"). Mr. Chu gave Fred to me and I put him on New Yorkey's head. That seemed like the best place for him. Then I paid Mr. Chu and said, "XieXie" (which is pronounced Shieh Shieh and means "thank you"), and we headed further downtown to the Brooklyn Bridge.

New Yorkey and I walk across the Brooklyn Bridge into the borough of Brooklyn all of the time. It's a good workout. Brooklyn used to be the fifth largest city in America until it became part of New York City. Now it's one of the trendiest places in the Big Apple!

It's autumn again and that means the leaves are changing color and beginning to fall. New Yorkey likes to roll around in the crackling leaves. I went into the garden to fetch him because we are going to a baseball game. I had a tiny baseball hat made for him. His ears stick out of the hat so that Fred can sit right between them without falling off. New Yorkey and I eat hot dogs in the stands while Fred hops in and out of the empty popcorn box.

It's fun going to baseball games, but I also like going to museums, Chinatown and the Statue of Liberty. When I asked Fred what his favorite place in the city was, he said, "Gribbitt, gribbitt" (which means the Brooklyn Bridge). New Yorkey, on the other paw, doesn't have a favorite place. When I asked him, he said, "Woof, woof, woof, woof, woof!" which means "It's too hard to pick just one favorite place in New York, especially for a New Yorkey!"